To Market, To Market

WRITTEN BY **Anne Miranda**

ILLUSTRATED BY **Janet Stevens**

Voyager Books
Harcourt, Inc.

Orlando Austin New York San Diego Toronto London

For information about permission to reproduce selections from this book, write
to trade.permissions@hmhco.com or to Permissions, Houghton Mifflin Harcourt
Publishing Company, 3 Park Avenue, 19th Floor, New York, New York 10016.

www.hmhco.com

Library of Congress Cataloging-in-Publication Data
Miranda, Anne.
p.   cm.
Summary: Starting with the nursery rhyme about buying a fat pig at
market, this tale goes on to describe a series of unruly animals that run
amok, evading capture and preventing the narrator from cooking lunch.
1. Nursery rhymes. 2. Children's poetry. [1. Nursery rhymes.]
I. Stevens, Janet, ill. II. Title.
PZ7.M657To   1997
[E]—dc20   95-26326
ISBN-13: 978-0-15-200035-6 ISBN-10: 0-15-200035-6
ISBN-13: 978-0-15-216398-3 pb ISBN-10: 0-15-216398-0 (pb)

SCP 33 32 31 30 29 28 27 26
4500634355

The illustrations in this book were done in acrylic, oil pastel,
and colored pencil with photographic and fabric collage elements
on 100% rag Strathmore illustration board.
The display and text type were Elroy.
Color separations by Bright Arts, Ltd., Singapore
Printed and bound by RR Donnelley, China
Production supervision by Stanley Redfern and Ginger Boyer
Designed by Lydia D'moch

Special thanks to Ideal Market in Boulder, Colorado
—J. S.

To my grandmother, Hattie Evans,
who used to bounce me on her knee
—A. M.

To Coleen Salley, who allowed me to
take her to market, to market;
to Shirley Sternola, for her encouragement;
and, of course, to Dorothy
—J. S.

To market, to market,
to buy a fat PIG.

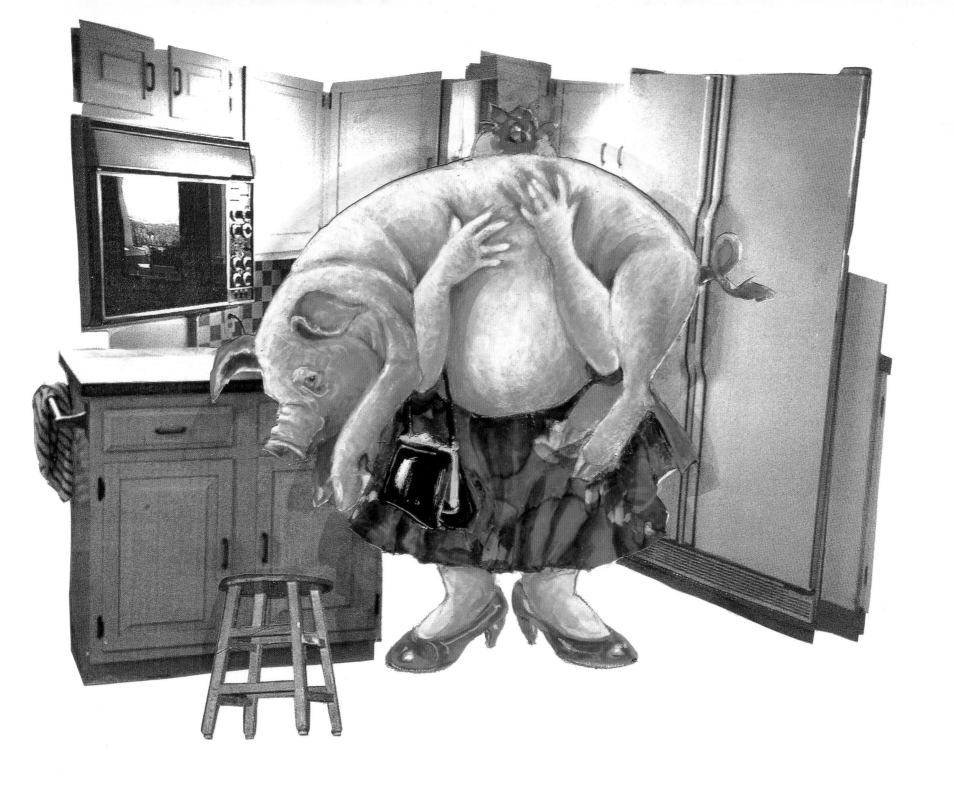

Home again, home again, jiggity jig!

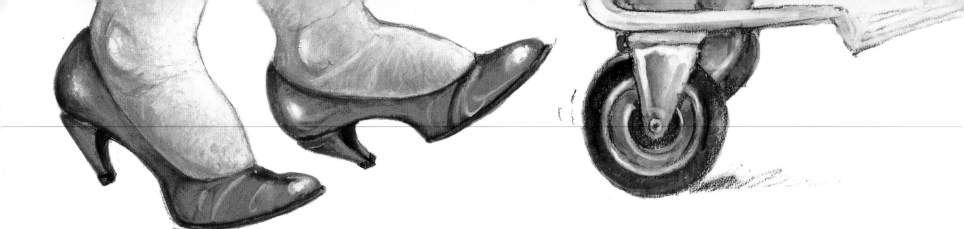

To market, to market,
to buy a red HEN.

Home again . . .

To market, to market,
to buy a plump GOOSE.

Home again . . .

Uh-oh!

The hen's
on the loose.

To market, to market,
to buy a live

TROUT.

Home again . . .

Uh-oh!

The goose
was let out.

To market, to market,
to buy a spring
LAMB.

Home again . . .

Uh-oh! Away the trout swam.

To market, to market, for one milking **COW**.

Home again . . .

Uh-oh! Where is that lamb now?

To market, to market, to buy a white **DUCK**

Now the cow disappeared,
and I'm out of luck!

To market, to market,
for one stubborn
GOAT.

The duck
flew the coop,
and the goat
ate my coat!

THIS IS
THE
LAST
STRAW!

The **PIG**'s in the kitchen.

The **LAMB**'s on the bed.

The **COW**'s on the couch.

There's a DUCK on my head!

The **HEN**'s in the cupboard.

The **GOOSE** is there, too.

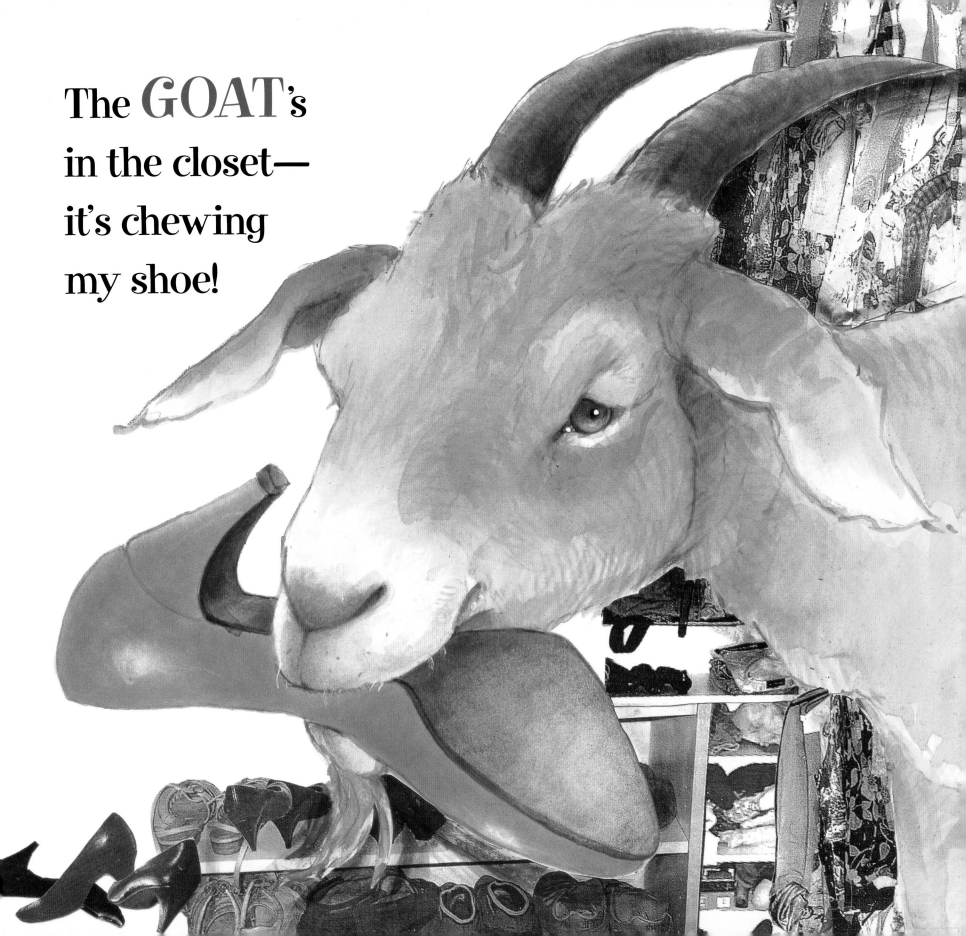

The **GOAT**'s in the closet— it's chewing my shoe!

The **TROUT**'s in the bathtub.
This place is a zoo!

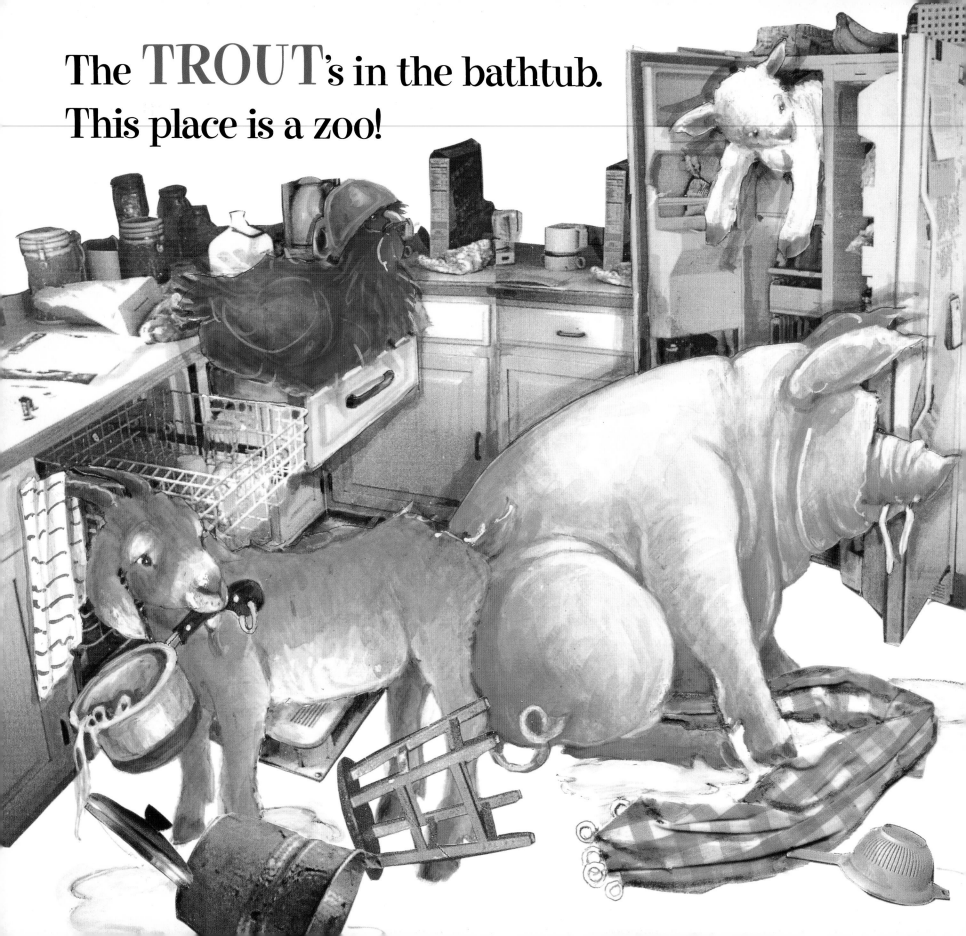

To market, to market,

to buy some POTATOES, CELERY, BEETS, and some ripe red TOMATOES,

some
PEA PODS

and

PEPPERS,

and GARLIC and SPICE,

a round head of **CABBAGE**,

a sack of
BROWN RICE.

Brown Rice

Add **OKRA**

and **ONIONS**

and one **CARROT** bunch.

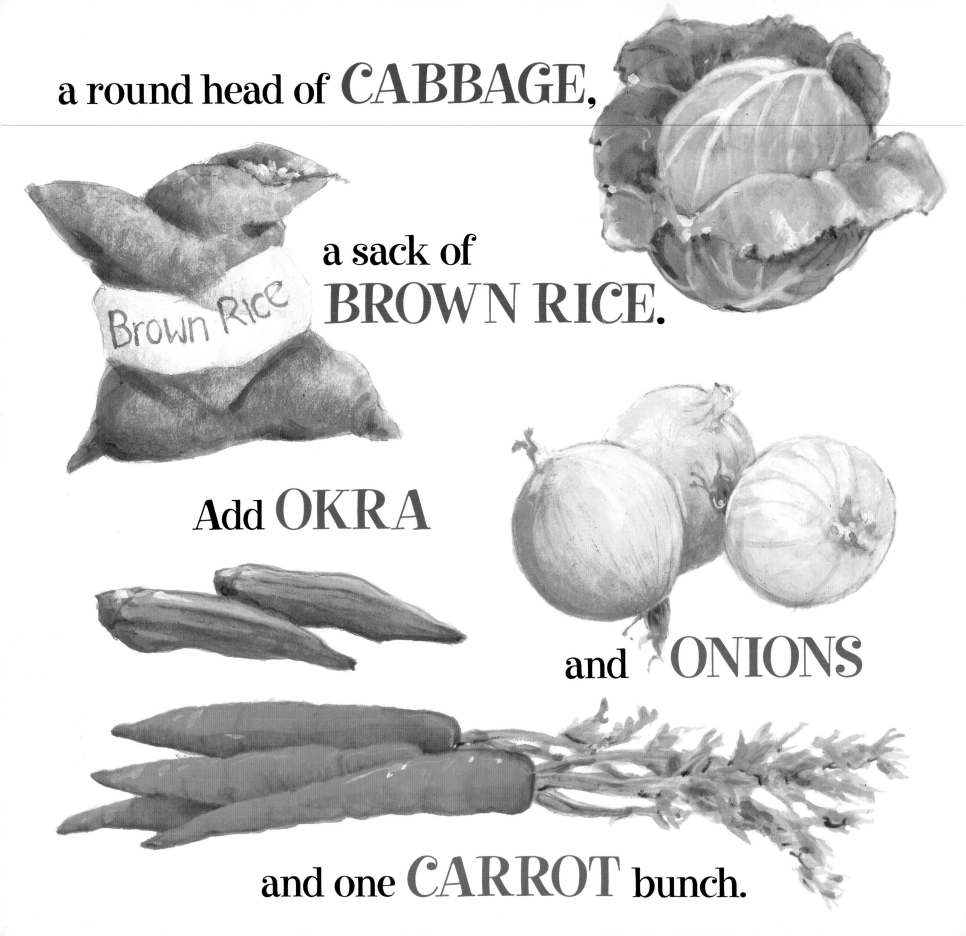

Home again, home again—

hot SOUP

for lunch!